W9-AAR-630

A Gift For:

_____

From:

_____

Copyright © 2012 Hallmark Licensing, LLC

Published by Hallmark Gift Books,
a division of Hallmark Cards, Inc.,
Kansas City, MO 64141
Visit us on the Web at Hallmark.com.

All rights reserved. No part of this publication
may be reproduced, transmitted, or stored in any
form or by any means without the prior written
permission of the publisher.

Editor: Megan Langford
Art Director: Kevin Swanson
Designer: Ralph Cosentino
Production Artist: Bryan Ring

ISBN: 978-1-59530-467-4
BOK1188

Printed and bound in China
SEP12

What Do Dragons Like to Eat?

By Megan Langford

Illustrated by Ralph Cosentino

Hallmark
gift books

What do dragons like to eat?
Is it salty? Is it sweet?

Potato chips and lemon pie.

Applesauce and ham on rye.

Peanut butter—jelly, too!
Bubblegum to pop and chew.

SLUUURP!

Root beer floats and chicken wings— dragons eat most anything!

Danby is a different beast.
The way he feels affects his feast.

Depending on his dragon mood,
he has a different favorite food!

**When Danby Dragon's feeling mad,
he starts to act a little bad.**

He breathes out fire and things get hot.
Look! S'mores! That hits the spot!

And if Sir Danby's feeling silly, the only food he wants is chili!

HA! HA! HA!

He starts to giggle, laughter grows,
and chili might come out his nose!

But sometimes Danby's feeling blue.
Then he only asks for stew.

Beef or fish, it doesn't matter—
just be sure to bring a platter!

And when he's cheered up all the way,
Danby craves a whole buffet.

He fills his plate to the tip-top,
then washes it down with soda pop!

When it's time to celebrate,
a slice of cake goes on his plate.

Instead of blowing candles out,
he lights them with his fiery snout!

What is Danby's favorite meal?
It doesn't matter how he feels.

When he's with his favorite guests,
a meal with friends is always best!

If you have enjoyed this book,
we would love to hear from you.

Please send your comments to:
Hallmark Book Feedback
P.O. Box 419034
Mail Drop 215
Kansas City, MO 64141

Or e-mail us at:
booknotes@hallmark.com